Cover design by Abira Das

"Akua's Masterpiece" written by Oladoyin Oladapo and Lynn Ma

Illustrated by Abira Das

Special thanks to our brilliant team and advisors: Olayinka Lawal, Ibironke Otusuile, Maimouna Siby, and Cindy Horng

Published
ISBN-13: 978-1-945623-05-9
ISBN-10: 1-945623-05-5

5-18
JF Ola

# Akua's Masterpiece

By Oladoyin Oladapo &

Lynn Ma

Illustrated by Abira Das

A GIRL TO THE WORLD BOOK

GHANA

To Toluwase, for keeping me young enough to write for children.

– Oladoyin

HOLLYWOOD

North America

Atlantic Ocean

Pacific Ocean

I am here
Ghana

South America

The World by
Akua

Arctic
Ocean

Europe

Asia

Pacific
Ocean

Indian
Ocean

Africa

Australia

Antarctica

Burkina
Faso

Benin

Tamale

Ghana

Cote d'Ivoire

Togo

Kumasi

Aburi

Atlantic
Ocean

Cape Coast

Accra

This is where
Akua lives.

# Ghana

is a beautiful country on the continent of Africa. People in the country speak lots of different languages. Ghana is known for its special kente fabric, cocoa, highlife music and so much more.

It is a bright sunny day in CAPE COAST, Ghana.

Akua's parents give her a brand NEW camera for finishing another year of school!

The very next day, they go on a road trip to Accra to visit the Memorial Park of the first president of Ghana: KWAME NKRUMAH..

Akua is very excited to test out her new CAMERA.

She takes PHOTOS of the Kwame Nkrumah statue and all the surroundings.

She can't WAIT to get back home!

When Akua returns home, she IMMEDIATELY prints out the photos on her printer. She prints so many photos that she loses count!

Akua lays out all of the photos
on her bedroom FLOOR.

I can't wait to show Yawo these photos!
Akua thinks to herself.

SUDDENLY, Akua has an idea.

She can make photo collages!

Kwame Nkrumah

Akua    Accra

The Afriyes

Ghana    Cape Coast

She takes out her BEST art supplies and

neatly pastes the photos on one big piece of paper.

Akua makes the most beautiful COLLAGE!
It has the photos from her trip,
short captions, and colorful decorations.

Holding it TIGHTLY in her hand,
Akua runs to Yawo's house.

She usually takes the BUS,
but today she cannot wait.

"Look, Yawo! I got a camera and made a collage out of the photos I took!" Akua excitedly tells Yawo.

"WOW! This is really cool!" Yawo replies.

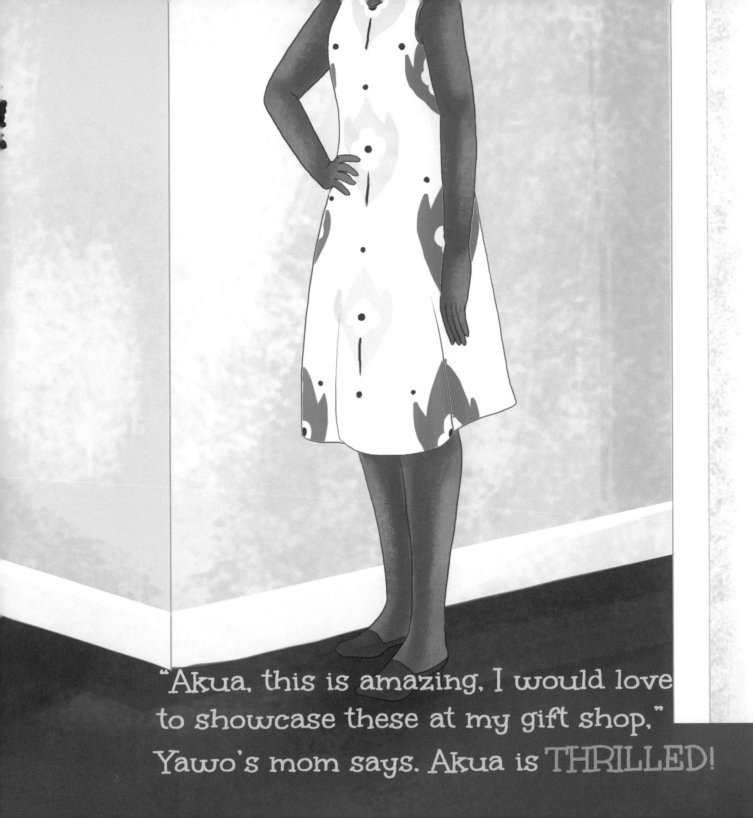

"Akua, this is amazing, I would love to showcase these at my gift shop," Yawo's mom says. Akua is THRILLED!

Then, Akua and Yawo sit down at the table for a SNACK. Yawo reaches for the plantain chips but accidentally KNOCKS over her mango juice. The juice spills all over Akua's collage!

"I'm so SORRY, I should've been more careful." Yawo exclaims.

"It's ok, but what do I do? It took me so long to make this," Akua says disappointedly.

Yawo's mom walks out of the room and returns with a paint set. "Girls, I have an IDEA," she says. Akua and Yawo look confused.

"We can splatter different colors all over the collage!" Yawo's mom suggests excitedly.

"What? Won't we ruin the collage even more?!" Akua is HORRIFIED!

"Oh no! We'll add more colors so the juice stains will seem like part of the collage, not an ACCIDENT." Yawo's mom explains.

"That's not a bad idea," Akua says. "LET'S DO IT!" Akua exclaims as she reaches over for the paint set. Akua and Yawo take all kinds of bright colors and splatter them all over the collage. Yawo makes one too.

After finishing, they look at the paint-splattered collages on the dining table. "These look pretty COOL," Akua says. Kwame Nkrumah's statue is pink, green, purple, and blue all over!

Akua and Yawo both carry the collages to Yawo's mom's gift shop. They help Yawo's mom hang them in the GIFT SHOP window.

A customer ask if the collages are for sale!

"They sure are. They are an Akua Afriye ORIGINAL!" replies Yawo's mom.

Maame's Gift Shop

"Who is AKUA AFRIYE?"
asks the customer.

"That would be me!"
Akua proudly interjects.

Akua and Yawo both high-five each other
for the successful TEAMWORK

An Akua Afriye Original

Girl to the World

Oladoyin Oladapo is a businesswoman and professional fun-haver. She loves to sing, dance, and create stuff, and when she's not doing that, she's watching Nigerian, Indian or Korean movies. She lives in Brooklyn, New York.

Lynn Ma is a student of life who is very excited to be a children's book author. She loves to roam the streets of New York City and eat very spicy food. Lynn lives in Brooklyn, New York

# Read Other
# Girl To The World
Books!

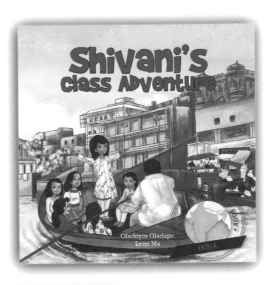

CPSIA information can be obtained
at www.ICGtesting.com
Printed in the USA
BVHW05n0243040418
512043BV00003B/55/P